YOUNG PEOPLES LIBRARY SERVICE

First published in 1997 by Franklin Watts

This paperback edition published in 1998

Franklin Watts
96 Leonard Street
London EC2A 4RH

Franklin Watts Australia
14 Mars Road
Lane Cove
NSW 2006

Editor: Suzy Jenvey
Series editor: Paula Borton
Designer: Kirstie Billingham
Consultant: Dr Anne Millard

A CIP catalogue record for this book
is available from the British Library.

ISBN   0 7496 3129 5 (pbk)
       0 7496 2591 0 (hbk)

Dewey Classification 365.02

Printed in Great Britain

Convict!

by
Julia Jarman

Illustrations by Liz Minichiello

W
FRANKLIN WATTS
LONDON • NEW YORK • SYDNEY

1

Wrongly Accused

Mary Catchpole hobby-horsed with the broom as she swept the cottage floor, and her sister Susan laughed.

"Get on with it, Mary, or mother will wallop you!"

"She'll have to catch me first!"

Mary was "jumping" the fender when their mother came in with a basket.

"Stop fooling, girl, and take the men their lunch. Run, now! They've been ploughing since dawn!"

Mary tugged at the latch on the door leading to the back yard, and started along the cart track towards the fields.

Twenty minutes later she was sitting on the plough-horse's broad back in the sunlight, watching her father and brothers eating their hunks of bread and cheese.

Mary loved horses. She loved it when the breeze lifted their manes and fluttered their feathery fetlocks.

She loved the jingle of the harness and the smell of sweat and leather.

This was her favourite part of the day.

It was on her way back that things started to go wrong. Mary was leaning across the gate to Hall Field gazing at the squire's new chestnut hunter, when she heard a scream.

"Help! Come quickly!" A maid was running out of the old wheelwright's cottage.

When Mary reached the kitchen, Mrs Denton lay stretched out on the cold stone flags of the kitchen floor. She looked very ill.

"Doc..." she gasped.

The doctor - of course!

The maid was dithering, so Mary took charge. Ordering her to fetch water from the pump for her mistress, Mary set off at a run.

Unfortunately, the doctor's was five

miles away. Even if she ran every step it would take an hour.

But then she had what seemed like a good idea.

Seconds later she was on the chestnut mare's back.

She must get to the doctor.

She must get to the doctor.

That was the only thought in her head.

She must get to the doctor.

She must get to the doctor.

Her thought kept time with the horse's hoofs as she raced through the countryside.

Going up Bishop's Hill she slowed a bit.

Then there was the town below her, with its twelve church towers and the river curving around it, but she didn't notice much of that.

The doctor - that was her only thought.

She kicked the horse faster.

However, it was market day. She had to weave her way around hay wagons, pig carts and carrier vans to reach Orwell Place where the doctor lived.

She was there at last! Leaning down from the horse's back, she rang the doctor's doorbell.

Doctor Stebbings praised Mary for acting so quickly. Then he harnessed up his cart and clattered off down the lane in a cloud of dust.

Mary patted the horse and felt relieved. But then her troubles really began.

A crowd of people had gathered in the doorway of the alehouse at the bottom of the lane, attracted by all the hoofbeats and shouting.

Mr Pryde, the squire's head man, pushed his way to the front of the crowd. He looked angry.

"Mary Catchpole! What are you doing with the squire's new hunter? Stealing's a transporting offence, you know!"

"I didn't steal it!" cried Mary.

"Tell that to the judge!" he said, stooping to examine the mare's leg.

"You've ruined this horse, galloping over the cobbles. There's a damaged tendon here."

He sent someone to fetch the constable.

The crowd were muttering and staring at Mary, who began to worry. People were saying the horse had cost a hundred guineas. Others were muttering that it might have to be shot.

The constable arrived and put chains round Mary's wrists. She tried to hold her head high as he walked her to the gaol.

She was not guilty.

She had *borrowed* the horse.

The constable handed her over to the gaolkeeper as silent faces stared at her from barred windows.

"Welcome to 'appy 'all," said a not-so-silent one.

"Silence, Nell!" shouted the gaoler. He opened the door of an empty cell.

Things went quickly from bad to worse. First, Mary was charged with *wilfully stealing and damaging a horse worth one hundred guineas.*

Then they said she would have to stay in gaol for fifty-seven nights - and days, of course - until her trial at the next Quarter Sessions.

Prison was dark and cold, but she was fortunate in a way. At least the gaol was clean.

And after a time, Mary was given some work to do sewing the blue calico uniforms they wore in the gaol.

But she was very lonely. That was part of the system - *Separate and Silent*, they called it.

Mrs Ripshaw, the gaoler's wife, told her she should use the time on her own to think

about what she'd done and repent. If she showed she was sorry at her trial, the judge might give her a lenient sentence.

"How long would a lenient sentence be?"

"Three years in gaol, or transportation for five years."

Mary didn't dare ask what a severe sentence would be.

To be locked up for three years! To be shipped to Australia for five!

Mary's mother came to visit on the night before the trial. She looked as if she'd been crying.

"We've got to move away, Mary. Your father's lost his job on account of what you did. The squire turned us out of the cottage this morning."

Mary felt dreadfully sorry and angry at the unfairness of it all.

"Promise me something, girl," said her mother. "Plead guilty at your trial. They say it helps your sentence if you show you're repentant."

"No," said Mary stubbornly.

She didn't feel sorry. She'd done a *good* thing. She had only *borrowed* the horse.

"I'd rather tell the truth, mother. Send word when you're settled. I'll be joining you there soon."

On the morning of the trial, Mary was taken from her cell when it was still dark and hand-cuffed to two other prisoners.

They travelled in the back of an open cart, and as it got light people could see them as they passed through the villages. Mary thought she would die of the shame.

The journey took five hours. It was late morning by the time the cart drew up around the back of the court building. The prisoners were taken down some steps and into a room like a cage.

Mary's case was the first to be called. Her hopes rose when Doctor Stebbings spoke up for her. She could hear the murmurs of approval all around the courtroom as the Doctor explained how her actions had probably saved Mrs Denton's life.

But they fell when Mr Pryde and then the squire himself took the stand.

There'd been a lot of horse stealing lately, the squire said. The lower classes were becoming too free with his property. They needed to be taught their place.

Mr Pryde said he had often seen Mary hanging around the horses' fields.

He'd even caught her in the stable yard once, patting the hunters. He said Mary had stolen the horse deliberately for a free ride, and she was using Mrs Denton's illness as an excuse.

Other witnesses were called - all tenants or servants of the squire - and they said the same thing.

Mary described exactly what had happened and said she was sorry she had lamed the horse.

Several more people spoke up in Mary's favour. They said she was honest, and worked hard.

The judge took a long time to make up his mind. Mary was beginning to feel quite hopeful.

But then he pronounced her guilty.

He said Mary had shown unbecoming pride in her actions. He said he was making an example of her, so that others would learn not to do the same thing.

Sentencing her to seven years' transportation, he ordered her to be taken to Portsmouth where a convict ship was waiting to sail.

2

Just a Number

"Number 78 - keep moving!"

The overseer's voice broke through the icy fog on the freezing dockside.

As she dragged her chained feet towards the convict ship, Mary remembered thinking that nothing could be worse than gaol.

But in gaol she'd had a name.

Now she was just a number.

It was on the papers that said she was a convict. It was on the arm of the grey uniform she wore. It was on the leg irons which had already made her ankles raw.

"Pull yer drawers down a bit and tuck 'em in!" Nell, number 77, called over her shoulder.

Nell, who had called out to Mary the day she'd arrived in gaol, was full of handy hints.

Mary had got to know her on the four-day journey to Portsmouth, and had learned that she'd stolen a handkerchief - to get money to feed her little brothers and sisters, she said.

"My mistress 'ad dozens of handkerchiefs. I didn't think she'd miss one. 'Ow many noses 'as she got, after all?" Nell had laughed.

Mary still didn't know what to think. Stealing was wrong, but Nell didn't seem one bit ashamed of herself. Very few of the other convicts did, either. Certainly not

Lizzie, Number 76, who had got caught stealing spoons - to get food for her family, she said. Her dad and brothers hadn't been able to earn enough money, now that farmers were paying their labourers so little.

Nell and Lizzie were talkative, but most of the convicts were as silent as Mary as they shuffled towards the *Sirius*, or stepped warily on to it.

It didn't look very safe.

But they were even more dismayed when they saw the barracoon in the hold of the ship where they were going to spend the next eight months.

How would they all fit in?

"By being packed like blooming sardines," Nell said.

"Or flipping jars of jam," said Lizzie.

Mary simply wished she could die there and then. Dark and airless, the prison stank already.

What would it be like when all hundred convicts were inside, packed three to a bunk?

What would it be like when it got hot?

When the buckets - four between all of them - were full of waste?

"Just think, our Clem paid for this!" said Nell.

She'd already told them about her older brother who had bought a ticket to Australia, to start his own farm there as a free settler. There was plenty of land in Australia, people said. Not like at home.

Nothing would stop Nell looking on the bright side. She was sure she was going to meet up with Clem eventually, even though she hadn't heard from him since he'd gone three years ago. She'd asked her family to get word to him that she was on her way.

But as Mary lay between Nell and Lizzie - the sea only inches away from her ear - she couldn't think of anything to look forward to.

Didn't convicts have to work like slaves for the free settlers? Or for the government?

Men in chain-gangs building roads, women in factory prisons sewing army uniforms?

If they got there. The ship looked old and it creaked a lot, shuddering when a bigger than average wave hit the sides.

What would it be like when they were at sea?

3

A Terrible Voyage

She was soon to find out.

Suddenly the roof of the barracoon shook as feet above moved quickly.

And there were shouts - about anchors being raised and main sails hoisted.

The fog had cleared, quite suddenly.

They didn't see, because you couldn't see anything from the barracoon. But as icy winds started to whistle through gaps in the woodwork, and the *Sirius* started to rock, they knew that the tide was coming in.

Shortly after that things on the ship felt different.

"We're on our way," said Nell.

Someone else said, "Good riddance to Great Britannia!"

But everyone else was silent - all thinking of the families they were leaving behind no doubt.

Mary tried not to think of hers - her mum and dad and sister Susan, her brothers Charles and Ned and the baby, little Tom - but she couldn't help it.

Would she ever see them again?

She thought of her friends, and of Doctor Stebbings and Mrs Denton who had both spoken up for her in court.

In the small bag of possessions tied round her waist, she had letters from them describing her good character. They would help her get a good position when she was free, they said.

Doctor Stebbings had said she mustn't lose hope. Lots of convicts eventually made good lives for themselves in Australia.

Mary tried to be optimistic. It helped a bit when the captain appeared in the doorway of the barracoon and said he was instructing the second mate to remove their leg irons. "On the strict understanding that you co-operate fully in the orderly running of the ship," he said. "Any bad behaviour will result in leg irons being restored and remaining for the rest of the voyage."

"Good old Cap'n Isaiah," said Nell, when at last they could stretch their legs.

But Lizzie said, "It's not because he's good, stupid. It's because he'll be in trouble if we're all lame when we get there and can't work. And we're not likely to try and escape are we?" They hadn't seen land for days.

"Why do you call him Isaiah, anyway?" she added. "Isn't his name Williams?"

"'Cos one of 'is eyes is *'igher* than the other, of course! Look at 'im next time," said Nell.

Lizzie laughed and so did Mary.

Nothing got Nell down - not their diet of ship's biscuit and water.

Nor the hours spent in the stinking barracoon - they were allowed only one hour on deck a day.

Nor the terrible seasickness which Mary

and nearly everyone else got as they crossed the Bay of Biscay.

As the ship reared from side to side, and the waves thundered and roared and water spurted through the scuttles, Nell did what she could to look after people. And she tried to keep the barracoon clear of vomit by sluicing it down with sea-water.

Her good humour kept them all going, and - when she stopped being sick - Mary really did start to feel hopeful too. Maybe things would turn out right.

They did see some amazing things - dolphins and whales and porpoises, and brilliant-coloured birds.

And one day Mary found Nell standing on her hands.

"What are you doing?" she gasped, because you could see Nell's drawers!

Fortunately all the sailors seemed to be asleep.

"Practising walking upside down," said Nell.

"Why?"

"We're going to the other side of the world, aren't we? So we'll have to."

Mary laughed, but it made her think. What would Australia be like? Some people called it the end of the world - but Nell, wonderful Nell, made it sound like an adventure.

So it was terrible when she became ill.

4

No Water

It couldn't have happened at a worse time.

For days the ship hadn't moved. It was blistering hot and there was no wind.

The sun blazed directly overhead and their water ration had been cut to half a pint a day. Nobody felt well - or looked well.

So Mary who had a terrible headache and blistered lips didn't notice that Nell was any worse than the others, till Nell suddenly flopped forwards. They were on deck at the time.

Then, of course, she sprang into action.

Lizzie helped Nell into the shade below.

Then Mary went to Captain Williams to ask for water.

It was obvious that Nell needed some desperately.

But to her amazement, he said no, not until the evening. Water had to be strictly rationed, he said, to make the supply - already low - last as long as possible. If they ran out they would all perish.

But he did agree to come and look at Number 77.

Mary led him to where Nell was lying, now thrashing her arms around.

"Clem...hankie...water..." She was obviously delirious.

The captain asked if she had a rash. It was hard to say. Her skin was so red anyway. So was everyone's.

He asked if she had vomited.

Lizzie said she had.

He said, "She'd better go into isolation. She may be infectious."

A few others had been taken ill, he said, and he'd got the crew to clear a space in the stores, near the bow, where they could be kept separate from the rest of the ship in case they passed on the disease.

There was quite a lot of space in the stores, after four months at sea. He ordered a sailor to take them there.

Lizzie helped Mary carry Nell.

The sailor kept his distance, they noticed.

He told them to put Nell inside the door and leave.

"Leave?" Mary counted six other convicts, including an old woman, all lying on the straw pallets.

The sailor said, "Come on."

Mary said, "But who's looking after them?"

He looked at her as if she was stupid.

"They can't look after themselves," said Mary.

Now it was obvious that the captain's only concern was to keep the ill convicts away from the rest.

The sailor said, "I've orders to take you back to the barracoon."

Mary refused to go. So did Lizzie.

Nell must be looked after. Her skin was burning hot and dry. If they couldn't give her a drink, they must cool her body somehow.

The sailor went off - that was something.

As quickly as they could, they took off Nell's prison dress. Then Mary stayed with Nell, fanning her, while Lizzie went to hang the dress over the side.

Their plan was to wrap Nell in the wet dress to bring her temperature down.

They knew better than to give her - or themselves - sea-water to drink.

But when Lizzie came back - with Nell's dripping dress - Captain Williams was with her.

"The punishment for disobedience is a return to leg irons," he said.

Mary said, "Put me in leg irons if you must, but let me stay."

He said he couldn't risk her life.

She said she'd risked her life already.

If Nell had got an infectious disease, she had probably got it too by now.

He said, "If you stay now, you stay in isolation with her for the rest of the voyage."

Mary agreed to that. So did Lizzie, but the captain said he wouldn't let two of them do it. His task was to deliver a full contingent of convicts fit for work.

But Lizzie was allowed to leave supplies outside the door each day. She brought their water ration that evening.

For the rest of the night and all through the

following day, Mary tended to Nell and the others as best she could.

But by the next nightfall the old woman had died.

When Lizzie brought their rations she said there was no water. However, a cloud had been sighted. The crew were spreading sails over the deck to collect every last drop of water if it did rain.

Mary told Lizzie about the old woman. Soon after she'd gone, a sailor appeared with a large canvas bag.

He told Mary to put the old woman's
body in it and leave the bag outside the door.
He said there were more bags if anyone
else died.

Later that day, Mary heard
hymn singing.

In the evening
Lizzie described
the funeral.

The old woman's body,
covered by a union jack, had been
slid down a plank into the sea, she said.

She asked how Nell was.

Mary said she was dreadfully still and quiet.

They were both silent then, thinking the same thing, till Mary said, "Nell's not going to die. I won't let her."

But all she could do was keep Nell as cool as she could, by sponging her body with sea-water.

Then in the middle of the night, she heard a new sound - of rain on canvas! - though she didn't realize it was that immediately.

Suddenly the ship was rocking violently.

Thunder rolled and cracked.

Round them a storm was raging.

Even so Lizzie managed to get fresh water to Mary and the invalids.

"Drink lots, Mary," Lizzie said. "I know you've been sharing your ration with Nell."

I'll bring more as soon as I can."

She did too - and more after that. For three days the storm raged, filling the water barrels and speeding the ship south. And slowly, day by day, Nell began to get better.

Five months later they caught a glimpse of land. Strange, purple-coloured hills and tall bright red geranium plants, as big as trees. Gradually the coastline curved to form a wide sandy bay.

Botany Bay.

5

A New Life

As the *Sirius* sailed towards the docking platform, Mary steeled herself for another test.

She saw people waiting. Government officials and free settlers looking for labour, the captain explained.

Long before you could see their faces, Nell scrutinized them.

"Poor Nell," said Lizzie. "She really thinks her Clem will be here to welcome her."

It was humiliating, shuffling on shore in leg irons.

It was even worse being inspected like cattle, as they moved towards an enclosure on the dockside.

"Number 27! Number 33!"

Some numbers were called out as people fancied the look of particular individuals.

Mary clutched her letters from Doctor Stebbings and Mrs Denton, but she noticed that people were mostly interested in what the convicts looked like.

Then she was brought to a sudden halt by Nell, who'd stopped walking.

"What's the matter?" Mary thought she'd fallen ill again.

Nell didn't answer. She was staring across at a brown-faced curly-haired man, standing on his own to one side of the crowd.

"Keep moving, 77!"

"Nell, move!" Mary urged.

Then another voice rang out, "Number 77! I'll have Number 77!"

As the curly-haired man stepped forward, a government official noted his request.

Mary's heart sank - so they were going to be split up. Her greatest dread.

They reached the enclosure.

Now consultations took place between officials and "purchasers".

A factory owner wanted thirty convicts. He took the first thirty in the line.

The head of the orphanage wanted three for domestic service.

She chose numbers 34, 39 and 45.

Then the curly-haired man claimed Nell, who had tears in her eyes. She was murmuring, "Clem, Clem. Is it really you?"

He muttered, "Quiet, Nell. If they know we're related, they might not let me have you."

She whispered, "Take Mary and Lizzie too. 78 and 76."

He said, "I need farm-hands. Men really."

She said, "They saved my life, Clem."

He said, "I'll have Numbers 78 and 76 too."

It was a bit of amazing good fortune. Word had reached Clem that Nell was on her way, but he'd come that day expecting a consignment of male convicts. He needed labourers for the farm he had started.

So Mary, who had always preferred

horsework to housework, started her new life in Australia on Clem Palmer's farm and soon became an excellent ploughwoman. She grew to like her new life in Australia.

When she had worked her sentence she decided to stay there, and eventually she became Clem Palmer's wife.

But she never forgot her family. She named her favourite farm horse Susan, after her younger sister.

CRIME and PUNISHMENT in Victorian Times

This book is based on the true story of Margaret Catchpole, who really was found guilty of horse-stealing and transported to Australia, where she served a seven-year sentence.

Victorian Punishments

In early Victorian times, crime was on the increase and the law dealt out harsh punishments to convicts - convicted prisoners. Until 1841 all murderers and some thieves received capital punishment - the death penalty - and were hanged. After 1841 only murderers were executed.

Thieves were sometimes punished by being flogged. Watched by the public, the constable would administer a number of lashes.

Prison

Many thieves - even if they stole something small, like a handkerchief - were punished by being sent to prison. Children were treated exactly the same as adults.

Some old prisons - like Newgate in London - were filthy and overcrowded. Men, women and children prisoners were all mixed together. In the new "model" prisons, like Pentonville and Ipswich, the Separate and Silent system was practised. Prisoners were kept in solitary confinement to think about their crimes and repent.

Transportation

This form of punishment - also called deportation - began in 1787 and continued through Victorian

times (1837-1901). It was seen
as a good way of ridding the
country of criminals, and of
developing Australia as Britain's
new colony using the criminals

as cheap labour. Over 108,715 convicts had been
transported by the time the system was abolished
in 1868!

Life in Australia

Convicts had to work for no pay. Their treatment
varied. Some, especially convicts who stole or got
drunk, were flogged, kept in chains, and given the
worst jobs. Others found to their surprise that they
were better fed than they had been in England.

Most convicts stayed on in Australia after their
sentence had ended, partly because they couldn't
afford the fare back, and
partly because they saw
Australia as a country
full of good opportunities.